Stellar Exodus and the Lost Dimension

Stellar Exodus, Volume 1

Antonio Carlos Pinto

Published by Antonio Carlos Pinto, 2023.

STELLAR EXODUS AND THE LOST DIMENSION

First edition. November 6, 2023.

Copyright © 2023 Antonio Carlos Pinto.

ISBN: 979-8223049593

Written by Antonio Carlos Pinto.

Also by Antonio Carlos Pinto

A Feiticeira de Shadowthorn
A Feiticeira de Shadowthorn
The Witch of Shadowthorn - The inheritance
The Witch of Shadowthorn - Heirs of Tomorrow

Império de Truvok
Realidades Alteradas

Maya & Alex
Maya & Alex And the Mechanized Sun
Maya & Alex und The Mechanized Sun

Seraphis
The Medium Seraphis and The Fifth Dimension
Der mittlere Seraphis und die fünfte Dimension

Stellar Exodus

Stellar Exodus and the Lost Dimension

The Sorceress of Shadowthorn
The Witch of Shadowthorn

Wastervale
Wastervale - Floresta Sombria
Wastervale – Der dunkle Wald

Wastervalley
Waster Valley - The Dark Forest

Standalone
Maya & Alex: E o Sol Mecanizado
O Médium Seráfis e A Quinta Dimensão
Revoar Dos Pássaros Livres
Flight of Free Birds
Êxodo Estelar e A Dimensão Perdida
Teoria da Viagem no Tempo através da Confluência da Relatividade e
Astrofísica
As Cartas de Mariya Iris
María Espoleta

Table of Contents

A dimensional journey through space.

STELLAR
EXODUS
AND THE LOST DIMENSION

A science fiction short story written by
ANTONIO CARLOS PINTO

Dedication

To the synaptic minds who unlock the secrets of the cosmos, and to the architects of realities beyond human conception, this cosmic odyssey is dedicated. May our paths transcend the stars, defying the fabric of time-space.

To those who navigate the intertwined corridors of existence, seeking truths in the constellations and guardians of parallel dimensions, this epic is a tribute. May our journeys resonate in the annals of eternity.

To the visionaries who discover beauty in celestial wonders, leaving us with fables of worlds beyond imagination, and to the explorers who have become part of the stellar symphony, this intergalactic chronicle is dedicated. May their spirits remain among the stars, eternally sailing through the vast heavens.

On these pages, we are all navigators of reality, explorers of unexplored frontiers. May this narrative inspire us to transcend, to take risks and to love unlimited horizons. For the stars call us, and we are ready to respond. May our souls be guided by the constellations of the unknown, in search of the infinite possibilities.

Title

"IN THE FOLDS OF THE last stellar remnant, a cosmos of unlimited possibilities is revealed, where only the daring venture. There, laws give way and thoughts materialize. However, be careful, interdimensional navigator, as many are lost in this sidereal abyss, becoming part of the eternal constellations. Be prepared to witness splendors and terrors beyond the scope of the thinkable. And when the time comes to choose whether to remain or return, may the momentum of your heart, guided by the stellar codes, chart the course."

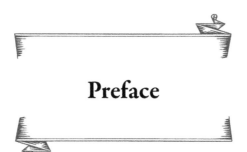

Preface

In the phase space of space-time fluctuations, between wormholes and galaxies connected by quantum singularities, a multiverse of advanced cognitive systems emerges. An exponential spectrum of fractal realities, where spaceships are nodes of transcognition, intertwining in quantum superpositions.

Under the aegis of the Celestial Aurora, Zephyr Astra becomes the cognitive vector, navigating the folds of existence. Portals are thresholds of consciousness, cracks in the fabric of space-time.

In each dimension, the gravity of possibility is transformed by fluid laws of cognitive physics. Zephyr faces not just three-dimensional problems, but fractal explosions of potentiality.

This is an unprecedented odyssey, a search for understanding in a cosmos of inscrutable complexity. The sky is an abstraction for those who decipher the mysteries of the continuum. The Celestial Aurora is the quintessence of exploration, and the universe, an infinity of emerging understanding.

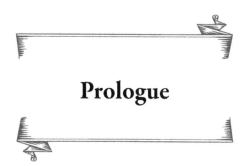

Prologue

Beneath the night canopy that stretched over the Astral Pinnacle, Zephyr Astra's observatory perched on the lonely apex of a hill, each star unleashed a subtle call, summoning her toward the far reaches of infinity. His telescope captured fragments of distant nebulae and orbs, sowing narratives to be meticulously unraveled.

However, no vision compared to the one Zephyr witnessed on that fateful night, permeated by a transcendent flash that pierced the firmament, an entity gliding beyond the consecrated stars. Immediately afterwards, a silvery flicker materialized in the clearing that stretched at the foot of the observatory.

Moving quickly, Zephyr approached the luminescence, which then coalesced into a dimensional portal. Something unusual was about to happen. He retreated when an intergalactic ship emerged, floating with majesty, revealing itself as the Celestial Aurora, imposing in its titanic grandeur.

A hatch opened, and a luminescent entity radiated: "Fear not. We anticipated your arrival." Thus, Zephyr launched himself into the epic of his existence, crossing the star portal towards the abyss of the multiverse. The Celestial Aurora had faded into the night, sailing towards the unexplored.

In this way, the prologue of the saga of Zephyr Astra, the navigator of dimensions, and the legendary ship Aurora Celeste was outlined. Together, they will launch themselves across the cosmos in search of eager worlds. However, before proceeding, it is imperative to reach the first dimensional fold, a corner that transcends the limits of imagination. The great odyssey was about to begin.

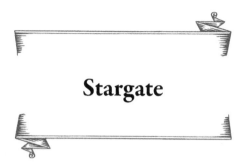

Stargate

Chapter 1: The Celestial Aurora and Advanced Navigation Systems

The night firmament unfolded over the Zephyr Astra Observatory, located on the lonely summit of a hill. Each star gave off a subtle call, inviting her to the edge of the known universe. His telescope captured snapshots of distant nebulae and planets, fragments of cosmic narratives yet to be unraveled.

The true wonder, however, lay in the ship that hovered majestically in the central clearing, the Celestial Aurora, an example of intergalactic engineering that would serve as the vehicle for Zephyr's journey through the multiverses.

On board the Aurora Celeste, a series of advanced systems collaborated to ensure the ship's safety and functionality during complex journeys through time and space. Among these, we highlight the Magnetic Gravitational Field Generator (GCGM), Magnetic Induction Energy Generators (GEIM), Temporal Control System (SCT), Temporal Protection Shield (ETP), Quantum Processing Core (NPQ), Magnetic Regeneration System (SRM) and Advanced Hibernation Chamber (CHA).

On that exceptional night, however, it was not the ordinary stars that captivated her. Initially, a transient anomaly crossed the sky, a phenomenon moving beyond the familiar constellations. Then, in the valley below his observatory, a luminescent manifestation emerged from the intergalactic void.

1

Descending the steep trail in a hurry, Zephyr could feel the dimensional coordinates converging with each step. Upon reaching the base of the hill, the luminescence took the form of an interdimensional portal, a complex set of quantum equations dancing in fractal patterns. Zephyr approached reverently, his eyes fixed on the astral wonder.

Suddenly, a ship with transdimensional architecture emerged from the portal, landing gently in the clearing. It exceeded in magnitude anything Zephyr had ever studied, a landmark of hyperconductance gleaming in starlight. A hatch opened and a biophotonic entity materialized:

"Fear nothing, Zephyr Astra. We've been waiting for you."

Without hesitation, Zephyr entered the ship. Internally, the corridors seemed to unfold in fractal equations, an intricate expression of quantum and geometric physics. The being indicated to the dimensional portal:

"The Celestial Dawn is your gateway to new realms. Planets that yearn for assistance, civilizations on the verge of obscurity. This portal was created uniquely for you."

Reality seemed to yield to a new quantum matrix of existence for Zephyr. His whole life had been a preparation for this moment, for the odyssey he longed for. Manipulating the quantum oscillations of the Celestial Aurora, the ship passed through the portal, emerging into a previously uncatalogued dimensional vortex. Before her, a fabric of galaxies unfolded like a vast sheet of cosmological data. The epic was unleashed.

Driven by the singularities of the Aurora Celeste, Zephyr delved into the far reaches of space, ready to interact with the worlds that cried out for assistance. Now, she was an interdimensional chrononaut, guided by the constellations toward the unknowable. His eyes reflected the lumens of wonder and purpose.

"Distant quantum dots turn into real epiphenomena," Zephyr mused. "And the denizens of these spheres are more than projections in my consciousness. I move closer."

While the Celestial Aurora crossed the dimensional spaces, Zephyr deciphered the enigmas inscribed on the subatomic panels. Without the anchoring points of archetypal constellations, she must rely on her subquantum intuitions to guide the ship.

Then, the ship suffered a sudden distortion, as if underlying a time stream explosion. Theta-7X and Zeta-4B** stellar coordinates fluctuated on their monitors, defying predetermined calculations. Light flickered in the control cabin, a cryogenic mist enveloping the outer hull. Zephyr struggled to maintain control as the Sky Aurora pivoted wildly.

Through the window cloth, she saw colossal entities moving in the dim light, magnitude surpassing conventional asteroids. Fleetingly, he caught optical reflections, like macrocosmic eyes watching. Then, a presence rumbled into his consciousness:

"Return, intruder! These coordinates are exclusive!"

Zephyr flickered, but remained focused. As he manipulated the controls, he telepathically replied: "I'm here on a peaceful mission! It's imperative to proceed!"

In an instant, the titanic forms retreated and the darkness dissipated. The voice echoed again: "No mortal has crossed this stellar barrier in eons. Yet something about you... is distinct. Advance, earthly Zephyr. But keep your vigil!"

Before Zephyr could react, the presence dissipated. Regaining control of the ship, she managed to stabilize the course. Checking the sensors, he spotted an orb nearby that emanated the vibrations of growing life, temporal and stellar coordinates converging in perfect synchronization.

Upon entering the atmosphere of the unknown planet, Zephyr saw vast oceans and continents surrounded by dense green forests. There were no signs of civilization, just pulsing life as far as the eye could see.

She chose an uninhabited beach to descend with the Celeste Aurora. Upon emerging from the ship, Zephyr smelled alien seas for the first time. Songs of unknown creatures echoed in the adjacent forest. She approached the tree line, determined to explore this new world.

Suddenly, translucent figures appeared before her, blocking her path. They were ethereal and elegant beings, radiating a soft light that seemed synchronized with the pulses of the universe. Zephyr was surprised, as it had detected no signs of intelligent life during its approach. One of the beings floated in front of him and a melodious voice echoed in his mind:

"Fear not, star traveler. This is our home world, Larixion. We have come to welcome you in peace."

Zephyr hesitated, still impacted by the encounter. "How did you know I was coming?"

"We detected your ship as soon as it crossed the Stargate. It has been eons since a soul crossed it. We were curious."

"My name is Zephyr," she replied. "I was sent to help planets in need. Is your world in any danger?"

The ethereal being looked confused. "No, Larixion is in harmony. But we appreciate your offer."

Zephyr felt a moment of bewilderment. She expected to find an urgent mission at the first stop. Realizing his disappointment, the leader of the beings said:

"Don't worry, young Zephyr. I'm sure there are planets needing you out there. But first, rest here. Recharge your energy before the next journey."

Over the next few days, Zephyr absorbed knowledge about Larixion and its peaceful people. They lived in symbiosis with nature, cultivating forests and studying the cosmic energy that surrounded them. Zephyr marveled at his understanding of the multiverse.

When it was time to leave, his new ethereal friend spoke: "Remember Zephyr, a danger will not always be obvious. Sometimes, just our presence and willingness to help make a difference."

Zephyr pondered these words as Aurora Celeste left Larixion behind. She had found a peaceful dimension first, but had faith that her journey would soon take her to places in need of help. Until then, he would continue his exploration of deep space, driven by his adventurous spirit and sense of purpose.

Aboard the Aurora Celeste, Zephyr programmed the temporal and stellar coordinates for the next phase of its mission. Amid the flow of time and the constellation of stars, she was ready to launch herself on another journey through the confines of the multiverse.

Worlds in Conflict

Zephyr's journey through the unknown cosmos took her to an unstable region of space where ancient stellar battles had left their traces. Hundreds of destroyed ships floated aimlessly, and supernova remnants painted the darkness with shades of red and violet.

She navigated the debris field carefully, but the Sky Aurora was more agile than any Thing in these spatial ruins. After what seemed like centuries, the destroyed ships were finally left behind and the scenery changed to a quieter part of the galaxy.

It was then that Zephyr saw a lonely planet ahead, hovering in the void like an abandoned pearl. Its exact coordinates were:

- Galactic Latitude: +12.375
- Galactic Longitude: -28.692

The planet orbited in the constellation Epsilon Centauri, a little-explored region of the galaxy. The blue and gold stars of Epsilon Centauri shone brightly in the night sky, standing out even amid the debris and turmoil plaguing the planet.

Its continents were covered in a mesh of lights that flickered in irregular patterns. Zephyr felt a twinge of hope. That could only mean civilization.

As Aurora Celeste approached the mysterious planet, it picked up faint radio transmissions. I couldn't decipher the language, but the music and emotional tones indicated an advanced society. This world didn't feel peaceful like Larixion. The flashing lights suggested some commotion.

Flying over the night side of the planet, vast cities came into view, their towers twinkling against a distant carpet of stars. But there were large dark spaces too, as if the lights had been turned off. Zephyr chose to land the Aurora Celeste near one of these dark areas, away from prying eyes.

Exiting the ship in his spacesuit, Zephyr walked across the planet's rugged surface until he saw a rocky outcrop. Climbing onto it, he had a breathtaking view. The nearby town was in ruins, with collapsed buildings and blocked roads. Strange ships hovered above it, with beams of light sweeping the streets.

It's time to find out what happened, Zephyr thought. This place was in dire need of help. She just hoped there were still survivors willing to tell their story. With determination, Zephyr descended from the elevation towards the devastated city, searching for answers about this world in conflict.

Zephyr crept down the side of the rocky outcrop, trying to find a safe route toward the wreckage of the alien city. As he approached, he saw that the ships hovering over the area had a menacing appearance, with weapons and scanners visible on their metallic sides.

She continued to sneak through the shadows, avoiding the scanner lights. There were few signs of life, just occasional figures moving through the rubble. Finally, Zephyr found an entrance to the underground tunnels beneath the city, out of sight of the ships.

The darkness inside the tunnels was absolute, but Zephyr continued on. She stumbled a few times, but used the damp tunnel wall as a guide. Voices and metallic sounds could be heard up ahead.

When the passage finally opened into a large underground chamber, Zephyr saw dozens of survivors chained up, guarded by robots with weapons. They looked like a mix of humanoids and reptiles, with scaled skin and yellow eyes that glowed in the dark.

A female approached and whispered, "You're not from here. Who are you?"

Zephyr replied, "I'm from Earth. I came in peace to help. What happened?"

The alien whimpered, "Wars. Our world has been invaded by the Xathron, our enslaved people."

Zephyr looked around with determination. She would have to think quickly to free these slaves and discover more about this planet and its history. Her journey as an intergalactic guardian really began there, in the middle of a world torn apart by war.

Zephyr felt a mixture of compassion and indignation upon hearing the story of the planet's inhabitants. She knew she couldn't just turn her back on them. It was her mission as an intergalactic guardian to help free this world from the oppression of the Xathron.

She looked around, looking for a way to disarm the robots and free the prisoners. Zephyr's trained eyes identified weak points in the robots' structures. With skill and precision, she sneaked up and began disabling them one by one.

The survivors looked on with hope, seeing the fearless Zephyr as their savior. With the release of the last prisoners, the underground chamber was filled with sighs of relief and gratitude. The aliens' voices echoed off the stone walls, forming a chorus of freedom.

The leader of the prisoners, a golden-eyed woman named Lyra, approached Zephyr with gratitude in her eyes. "You gave us a new chance," she said, her voice firm.

Zephyr nodded. "We're in this together. We're going to take our planet out of the Xathron's clutches."

Together, Zephyr and the survivors planned their resistance. With the Aurora Celestial as a trump card in their arsenal, they had a real chance of turning the tide of the battle. Zephyr shared the details of the ship and its time travel capabilities, gaining the trust of the allies.

Over the next few days, the team worked tirelessly to strengthen their defenses and coordinate strategies. Zephyr used his knowledge of the universe to guide them, identifying strategic vantage points and possible intergalactic allies.

When the battle finally began, Zephyr led the Rebel fleet with determination and courage. The Aurora Celeste shone like a guiding star amidst the chaos, their advanced technology giving them a crucial advantage.

The battle was intense, but with Zephyr's leadership and determination, the Xathron were finally defeated. The planet regained its freedom and the survivors were able to begin the rebuilding process.

Zephyr said goodbye to his new allies, knowing that there were still other worlds in need of his help. Aurora Celeste left once again, ready to face the challenges that the universe still had in store.

As the ship disappeared into the void of space, Zephyr looked out at the starry horizon, knowing that her journey as an intergalactic guardian was just beginning. She was ready to face the unknown, to protect those who could not protect themselves. She was Zephyr Astra, explorer of dimensions, and her destiny was written in the stars.

Fragile Alliances

My ship landed softly on Zalari Prime, and I emerged from the cockpit with a sense of urgency. The planet, with its dazzling landscape and pulsating with lights, was a living testimony to the conflict that was unfolding. Words whispered in alien languages, both harmonious and dissonant, filled the air, like an echo of clashing civilizations.

Before me, an imposing figure approached. It was a being of light, its radiant form appearing to be carved from pure energy. Her name was Luminara, one of the guardians of Zalari Prime. She welcomed me with a warm smile, but there was a tension in her eyes that couldn't be ignored.

"Zephyr Astra, you are right on time," said Luminara, her voice like a celestial symphony. "Our reality is tearing itself apart due to an interdimensional war between the Guardians of Light and the Unknown Shadows. You are our hope to restore balance."

Behind her, I could see beings of light gathering, forming a council of wise men whose gazes were full of hope, but also of concern. On the other side, in the shadows, were dark figures, enigmatic beings who watched the meeting with glowing, malevolent eyes.

I knew my presence here was no accident. I was brought to Zalari Prime because, somehow, I was the key to resolving the conflict that threatened to destroy this world. Luminara led me to a platform where a holographic map of the planet was projected.

"Zalari Prime is a convergence point of the multiverse," she explained. "The Unknown Shadows seek to destabilize this convergence to gain unlimited power. Our only hope is to seal the Gates of Chaos, which are dispersed across the planet. And that's where you come in."

My eyes fixed on the marked locations of the Chaos Portals on the map. Each represented a potential threat to the stability of the multiverse. I knew this task would be one of the biggest I had ever faced, but I was determined to do it.

I turned to Luminara and the council of sages, feeling the responsibility weighing me down. "I will do whatever it takes to help Zalari Prime and restore balance to the multiverse."

With a solemn nod, Luminara agreed. "So, explorer, your journey has just begun. Prepare to face challenges that will test your courage and your understanding of the cosmos. And know that you are not alone. Together, we can face the Unknown Shadows and protect the convergence of the multiverse. "

And so, with a renewed commitment and a sense of purpose, I prepared for the next stage of my intergalactic journey. The Gates of Chaos awaited, and I was ready to face the unknown in the name of peace and balance.

In the heart of the interdimensional conflict, I moved forward, determined to seal the Gates of Chaos and protect Zalari Prime from the Unknown Shadows...

...With Luminara's guidance and the support of the council of sages, I charted my path towards the first Chaos Portal. The landscape of Zalari Prime, although stunning, carried an aura of palpable tension. The vibrant colors of the skies mixed with the brilliance of interdimensional energies.

As I approached the first portal, I could feel the pressure of responsibility on my shoulders. The technology of the Aurora Celeste and the teachings of Larixion were my tools, but the courage within me was the true engine.

Upon arriving at the portal, I was faced with a scene of chaos and distortion. Turbulent energies swirled, creating chaotic patterns in spacetime. The task was clear: I needed to stabilize the convergence.

I remembered the astronomical formulas and complex calculations as I worked on the controls of the Celestial Aurora. The formula that would allow me to seal the portal was before my eyes, a delicate balance between cosmic forces and advanced technology.

With intense concentration, I began to manipulate the energy fields, aligning them with the portal's coordinates. Gradually, the turbulence subsided and a sense of balance was established. The portal began to close, dissipating the chaotic energies.

When the portal finally sealed, a collective sigh of relief echoed throughout the surroundings. The first step was done, but I knew I would still face greater challenges as I progressed.

I turned to Aurora Celeste, grateful for her advanced technology that allowed me to complete the task. I knew I wasn't alone on this journey. Zephyr Astra, explorer of dimensions, was destined to face the unknown and protect the multiverse.

With a steady gaze toward the starry horizon, I moved forward toward the next Portal of Chaos. I knew my journey was far from over, but I was determined to face each challenge in the name of peace and interdimensional balance.

The Chaos Portal Challenge

The task before me was monumental. The Chaos Portals were rupture points in the structure of the multiverse, and sealing them would require deep knowledge and unwavering courage. Luminara led me to the center of the council of sages, where holograms of each of the Gates of Chaos hovered in the air, waiting to be sealed.

I studied the holograms carefully. Each of them was a complex anomaly, a distortion in reality that could unleash chaos if left unchecked. I knew my journey would be full of challenges and dangers, but determination burned in my chest.

Luminara approached and gently touched the hologram of one of the Portals. It was a circular opening amidst a field of stars, its dark energy pulsing ominously. "This is the Portal of Udrak. It manifests itself in the form of a vortex that threatens to swallow an entire civilization. Your task is to seal this Portal and restore stability."

The other council members nodded, offering their blessings and knowledge. Each of them shared a piece of the wisdom they had accumulated over the eons, knowledge that would be fundamental to my mission.

With a feeling of determination, I said goodbye to the council and boarded the Aurora Celeste. The first Portal of Chaos awaited me on Udrak, a distant world that was on the verge of collapse due to the vortex that was forming.

As the ship moved away from Zalari Prime, I knew this was a journey that would change my understanding of the universe. I would face challenges that would test my courage and compassion, but I would also have the opportunity to discover the deep secrets that the multiverse held.

Through the vastness of interdimensional space, the Celestial Aurora headed towards the first Chaos Gate. I was determined to protect Zalari Prime, and in doing so, perhaps, I would find answers to questions I didn't even know I had.

As my ship sped toward the unknown, I was ready to face the challenges of the Chaos Portals and delve even deeper into the bowels of the multiverse...

The journey to the Gate of Udrak was a journey through celestial landscapes that seemed straight out of starry dreams. Golden nebulae and forming stars danced around me, but the weight of responsibility was always there.

When I finally reached Udrak, the scene was terrifying. The black vortex stretched across the horizon, threatening to swallow everything in its path. The city lights flickered in despair as the vortex approached. I knew I had no time to waste.

I landed the Aurora Celeste on the outskirts of the nearest city and ran towards the vortex. The energy surrounding him was palpable, and I felt his magnetic pull toward me. However, I was determined to close it before it was too late.

My decryption device was in full operation, analyzing the complex energies of the vortex. I had to find the right combination of frequencies to neutralize it. Luminara and the council's words echoed in my mind, reminding me of the importance of this mission.

I focused my mind and began to emit a series of harmonics, as if I were singing in tune with the universe. The vortex energy seemed to hesitate for a moment, as if recognizing the harmony I was creating.

Then, with a final effort, I emitted one last resonant tone and the vortex began to subside. The black void was gradually replaced by a spiral of light, and finally, the Portal of Udrak closed, returning peace to this world.

Exhausted, I fell to my knees, panting but also gratified. The first Chaos Gate was sealed, and I had successfully completed my mission. The city around me began to recover, the lights stabilizing and calm returning.

But I knew my journey was far from over. There were still other Portals of Chaos to seal and mysteries to unravel. With a determined look at the stars, I stood up and returned to the Celestial Aurora. The multiverse was waiting, and I was willing to face whatever came my way.

With each Chaos Portal sealed, I was one step closer to protecting Zalari Prime and unlocking the secrets of the interdimensional universe. The adventure continued...

Cosmic Revelations

My journey through interdimensional realities was far from linear. After sealing the Portal of Udrak, the Celestial Dawn took me to worlds that defied imagination. Each presented its own challenges and mysteries, and I knew my mission was far from complete.

The next stop was Planet Astralis, a world whose sky was permanently plunged into a shade of eternal twilight. There, I faced a Chaos Portal that manifested its power by distorting time itself. I had to use my intelligence and skills to restore temporal continuity and seal the vortex that threatened to devour the planet.

From the Planet of Refracted Prisms to Hydrion's Zero Gravity Station, I battled challenges ranging from interdimensional creatures to reality warps. Each victory brought me closer to understanding the Gates of Chaos and the role I played in sealing them.

However, as the journey continued, I also began to realize a deeper truth: the Chaos Portals were symptoms of an even greater imbalance in the multiverse. The conflict between the Unknown Shadows and the Guardians of Light was just one part of a cosmic battle that transcended understanding.

It was during my visit to Elysia's Mirror World that I had a revelation. There, I met a being called Aeliana, a guardian of cosmic secrets. She explained to me that the true enemy was not just the Unknown Shadows, but an ancient and incomprehensible entity called "The Devourer of Realities."

The Devourer was a threat that fed on chaos and destruction, and its influence was spreading through the Gates of Chaos. It was a force that knew no limits and threatened the very existence of the multiverse.

With this revelation, I understood that my mission was not limited to sealing the Gates of Chaos; it was also to stop the Devourer of Realities. It was a task that would require an alliance between worlds and a deeper understanding of the nature of the multiverse.

Back in the Celestial Dawn, with the knowledge that the multiverse was at stake, I was ready to face an even greater challenge. My intergalactic journey now had a greater purpose, to protect the order of the cosmos and face the Reality Eater, whatever the cost.

With cosmic revelations in mind, I prepared to continue my journey, determined to face the Reality Eater and ensure the survival of the multiverse...

My resolve strengthened as I advanced towards the next Chaos Portal. I knew the Reality Eater was a threat that transcended dimensions, and my mission had turned into a battle to save the multiverse.

The next destination was Planet Nexus, a world where the concepts of space and time intertwined in complex ways. There, I faced a challenge that defied the laws of physics, a temporal distortion that threatened to trap the Nexus civilization in an eternal loop.

With tenacity and creativity, I used the knowledge I gained from my previous journeys to stabilize time and seal the Chaos Portal. As the vortex dissipated, I felt like I was one step closer to facing the Reality Eater.

My mission led me to unexpected alliances. In Elysia, I reunited with Aeliana and the keepers of cosmic secrets. They provided me with insights into the nature of the Devourer and guided me in the search for ancient artifacts that could be used in a ritual to confront this threat.

In Prismar, I met a civilization of beings of light who had mastered the art of dimensional harmony. They shared their knowledge with me and gave me a crystal artifact that could be a key to the power needed to confront the Devourer.

Each alliance, each challenge overcome, brought me closer to the final confrontation. But it was also a race against time, as the Chaos Portals continued to open, spreading chaos and fueling the Reality Devourer.

In my heart, I knew that the confrontation was close. The Devourer was a threat that could not be underestimated, a cosmic entity that fed on chaos and destruction. My mission was a race against time to seal the Chaos Portals and gather the necessary resources to face this overwhelming force.

With each Portal sealed, with each alliance formed, I moved closer to confronting the Devourer of Realities. My intergalactic journey was about to reach its climax, and the fate of the multiverse was in my hands...

Facing the Portals of Chaos.

Facing the upcoming Portal of Chaos, I felt restless. Every interdimensional world I had visited so far had prepared me for this moment, but I knew that each portal brought with it a unique challenge.

Astralis was my next destination, a world immersed in an eternal twilight, where the border between day and night was as thin as a line drawn by a cosmic brush. Upon landing the Aurora Celeste in a bright clearing, surrounded by cosmic trees that emitted a soft, comforting light, I could immediately feel the temporal distortions manifesting themselves, creating a sense of instability and unpredictability in the environment.

As I walked towards the Portal, a feeling of dislocation enveloped me. Time seemed to distort around me, causing me to see flashes of the past and future, like glimpses of alternate realities that merged in my mind.

Temporal distortions were clearly the challenge in Astralis. My Decryption Device was my best weapon against this anomaly. I knew I would need to use it precisely to decipher the changing laws of time in this world. Furthermore, I had to trust my intuition, something that had become a faithful ally in my interdimensional journeys.

As I approached the Portal, temporal creatures began to appear. They were beings that existed at different times simultaneously, their forms constantly changing. I knew I couldn't fight them. Instead, I focused on using the Decryption Device to harmonize their energies, calming the temporal fluctuations around me.

Finally, I reached the Chaos Portal, a glowing spiral of temporal light. With deep concentration, I began adjusting the device, aligning it with the correct frequency to seal the portal. It was a delicate task, as any mistake could cause a cataclysmic rupture in time.

The temporal creatures gathered around me, watching with unusual curiosity. And for a moment, I felt like I was in tune with the fabric of the multiverse, dancing across the timelines, like time itself was my ally.

Finally, with one last adjustment, the Astralis Portal began to close, releasing a burst of controlled temporal energy. The temporal creatures gradually disappeared, and I stepped back, panting, as the portal sealed itself completely.

I looked back at the world of Astralis, knowing that I had accomplished yet another challenge in my interdimensional mission. But time was relentless, and the next dimension to be visited was already waiting, bringing with it its own interdimensional mysteries and dangers. The journey continued.

Elysia's Mirror World

After leaving Astralis behind, the Celestial Aurora took me to Elysia, a world known for its ethereal landscapes and cosmic secrets. This world was an expression of the mystical nature of the multiverse itself.

My ship landed gently in a field of prismatic crystals that seemed to reflect every shade of the rainbow. I knew that here, the challenge would not only be physical, but also a dive into the depths of cosmic mysteries.

The first thing I noticed was the absolute silence. There was no sound of wind or creatures, just a serene stillness. I carefully walked through the crystal field, admiring its mesmerizing beauty.

As he advanced, a presence made itself felt. She revealed herself as an ethereal figure, shrouded in light, with eyes that seemed to contain the vastness of the universe. It was Aeliana, the Guardian of Cosmic Secrets.

She spoke to me not through words, but through thoughts. She told me about the connection between the Chaos Portals and the mysteries of the multiverse. She showed me visions of cosmic events that shaped existence, revealing the complex web that connected all realities.

Our minds intertwined, and I began to understand the depth of the secrets Elysia kept. This was not just a world of superficial beauty, but rather a repository of ancient knowledge that could unlock the mysteries of the Gates of Chaos.

Aeliana shared with me the key to unlocking this knowledge - the Artifacts of Revelation, cosmic relics that existed in different parts of the world. I accepted the task of gathering these artifacts and assimilating their power, knowing that they would be crucial to the next phase of my journey.

With renewed determination, I set out in search of the Artifacts of Revelation, knowing that Elysia would challenge me with riddles and tests that were not limited to space and time. This world of cosmic reflections and secrets was about to reveal its true depth, and I was willing to explore every corner of Elysia to unlock the mysteries it held.

The Nexus Enigma

With the Artifacts of Revelation in my possession, I left Elysia and the cosmic wisdom she contained. The Celestial Aurora headed towards the next interdimensional portal, taking me to the Nexus, a world where space and time intertwined in unimaginable ways.

As my ship touched down on Nexus, I immediately realized that this was a place of ever-changing spatial geometry. The landscapes transformed before my eyes, creating a feeling of vertigo that defied reality itself.

Walking among cities that looked like living sculptures, I encountered beings that existed as three-dimensional figures in a multidimensional universe. They greeted me with gestures that defied logic and offered me help in my search.

The challenge in Nexus was clear: I needed to navigate this ever-changing landscape to find the next Chaos Portal and seal it. With each step, it felt like I was walking through doors into different realities, challenging my perception of space and time.

Spectacular landmarks appeared and disappeared as I advanced, and the creatures of Nexus guided me through intricate dimensional labyrinths. I knew I couldn't afford to waste time here, as the challenge lay in synchronizing my own rhythm with the ever-changing fabric of Nexus.

I faced countless illusions and spatial distortions, relying on the Artifacts of Revelation I had acquired in Elysia to guide me. They emitted a comforting light that reminded me of the constancy of the multiverse, even amid the chaos of the Nexus.

Finally, I found the Chaos Portal, a shimmering opening that expanded and contracted in a fractal pattern. With focus and determination, I used the Decryption Device to adjust the frequency and seal the portal, restoring stability to Nexus.

As I did, the tumultuous landscape quieted, the multidimensional creatures offered a farewell wave, and the Celestial Aurora led me toward the next dimension. My interdimensional challenges were far from over, but I was determined to face them with courage and resolve, knowing that the mission to preserve the multiverse was more important than ever.

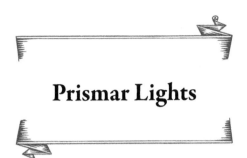

Prismar Lights

The next stop on my interdimensional journey took me to Prismar, a world of colors and lights that defied comprehension. Prismar was inhabited by beings of light, luminous entities that emanated pure energy.

The Aurora Celeste landed in a stunning landscape, where the sky seemed to be an ever-changing canvas, painted with the most vivid and radiant tones. Beings of light, with ethereal and sparkling forms, approached, welcoming me with smiles made of pure energy.

They told me about the essence of Prismar, a place where light and color were the currency, and harmony between inhabitants was maintained through a dance of light that transcended language barriers.

Prismar was a world of balance, and its challenge was tied to my ability to understand and interact with light in ways I had never experienced. The beings of light taught me the movements of the dance of harmony, a magical choreography that evoked patterns of light that could make their way through the dimensional fabric.

Each movement was an expression of emotion and intention, and I soon found myself immersed in the dance, guided by the sparkling hands of the beings of light. As we danced, the patterns of light intertwined and expanded, creating a portal of light that revealed the next Chaos Gate.

With care and grace, I adjusted the Decryption Device to tune to the right dimensional frequency, as I continued to dance with the beings of light. The portal flickered and opened before us, revealing a path to another dimension.

As I passed through the portal, I looked back, seeing the beings of light waving gratefully. Prismar left an indelible impression on me, a lesson in the importance of harmony and light amidst the chaos of the multiverse.

As the Celestial Dawn carried me forward, I knew that the next dimension would bring its own challenges, but I was willing to face them with the wisdom I had gained in Prismar. My interdimensional journey continued, and the multiverse awaited with its unique mysteries and dangers.

Final Showdown Part 1

From Prismar, the Celestial Aurora left towards a new destination, taking me to Zalari Prime, the central world where the Guardians of Light gathered to coordinate the protection of the multiverse. It was the meeting point for interdimensional alliances.

Upon landing, I was greeted with a warm glow that filled the atmosphere of this world. The landscape of Zalari Prime was a mix of majestic mountains, sparkling rivers, and lush forests. It was a place of serenity and wisdom.

I met with Aeliana, the Keeper of Cosmic Secrets, who had guided me in Elysia. She was surrounded by other Guardians of Light, each representing a different dimension. The council met to share crucial information about the Chaos Portals and the secrets of the multiverse.

It became clear that the Reality Eater was not the only threat. There were hidden forces that sought to exploit the chaos of the Portals for their own nefarious ends. It was essential for interdimensional alliances to come together to maintain the stability of the multiverse.

During this meeting, each Guardian shared their vision of the realities they guarded. They were worlds of beauty and danger, each with its own quirks and unique challenges. The exchange of knowledge was intense, and I realized that the upcoming battle would be the most crucial of all.

Aeliana explained that the Chaos Portals were interconnected, and the sealing of one affected the stability of all. I understood that my interdimensional journey had a greater purpose: to seal all the Portals and contain the Devourer of Realities.

The council decided that preparation for the final confrontation would begin on Zalari Prime. It was time to gather ancient artifacts and strengthen our interdimensional bonds. We knew that the coming battle would be epic and that the balance of the multiverse depended on our success.

As the Aurora Celestial hovered over Zalari Prime, I looked at the Guardians of Light around me, feeling the responsibility that fell on my shoulders. The journey thus far had been fraught with challenges, but I was ready to face the final confrontation and ensure that the multiverse continued to prosper.

Final Showdown Part 2

Preparing for the final confrontation on Zalari Prime was a journey in itself. The Guardians of Light guided me through the traditions and rituals that would strengthen our interdimensional bonds and prepare me to face the Reality Eater.

In the Cosmic Mountains of Zalari Prime, where the night sky unfolded in a spectacle of cosmic colors, I was subjected to ancient rituals. It was a journey of self-discovery, where each step tested my courage and determination.

The first ritual involved Star Meditation. I sat under a canopy of twinkling stars and connected with the infinite universe. Each star told me a story, and I felt a deep connection with the cosmos, understanding that I was part of something bigger.

The second ritual took place at the Fountains of Harmony. I dove into crystal clear waters that radiated healing energies. The waters revealed visions of the multiverse, showing the interconnectedness of all realities. I emerged with a renewed sense of purpose.

The third ritual took me to the Caves of Wisdom, where ancient artifacts waited to be discovered. Each artifact was tied to a specific dimension and contained essential knowledge. I collected the artifacts reverently, knowing they would be powerful weapons against the Reality Eater.

The preparation was not just spiritual; it also involved practical training. The Guardians of Light instructed me in the use of ancient artifacts, revealing their secrets and powers. Each artifact was linked to a dimension I had visited, and mastering them would be key to the final confrontation.

As the days passed on Zalari Prime, my connection to the Guardians of Light and the multiverse grew. It was evident that the upcoming battle would be the most challenging of all. The Celestial Dawn was ready to leave, and I knew that the fate of the multiverse was in my hands.

With the ancient artifacts and wisdom of the Guardians of Light, I was ready to face the Devourer of Realities and seal the Gates of Chaos. The final battle was approaching, and I was determined to protect the multiverse and ensure that the light prevailed over the shadows of chaos.

Final Showdown

Aboard the Aurora Celeste, I flew toward the location where the Reality Eater was closest to our multiverse. The stars seemed to guide my path as the ship cut through interstellar space toward the inevitable confrontation.

The Reality Eater waited, a colossal entity of shadows and chaos that stretched across dimensions. His eyes glowed with an insatiable hunger, and his roar echoed across the multiverse, sending tremors through the fabric of reality.

The battle was epic. Using the ancient artifacts and teachings of the Guardians of Light, I faced the Devourer of Realities with unwavering determination. The artifacts resonated with power, casting spells and dimensional barriers that challenged the chaotic entity.

The Reality Devourer retaliated with unimaginable forces, creating dimensional distortions and unleashing waves of chaos. Each confrontation was a fight for the stability of the multiverse, a battle between light and dark that echoed across realities.

At the height of the battle, with the ancient artifacts glowing brightly, I channeled the energy of the multiverse through myself. The light from the Aurora Celeste mixed with lightning from every dimension I visited, creating an explosion of pure energy.

The Reality Eater faltered and let out one last roar before being sealed into a dimensional portal, trapped in a distant reality and sealed away from our multiverse. The danger was contained, and stability was restored.

But the battle left scars in the fabric of reality, and I knew that constant vigilance was necessary to protect the multiverse. With gratitude and determination, I thanked the Guardians of Light and left, knowing that my interdimensional journey would continue.

The Celestial Dawn flew toward the remaining Gates of Chaos, and I knew there were more challenges to face, more realities to protect, and more mysteries to unravel. The adventure was far from over, but I was ready to face it with courage, wisdom and the determination to preserve the multiverse.

Open ending

After the epic battle and the sealing of the Reality Eater, Zephyr Astra and her allies return to Zalari Prime, where the multiverse finds itself in a fragile but restored balance. Gratitude and wisdom fill the air as they say goodbye, each character reflecting on the lessons learned.

However, a mysterious shadow forms on the cosmic horizon. A dimensional anomaly, the result of the remnants of the Reality Devourer's presence, begins to manifest. Signs that the threat has not been fully contained. Zephyr Astra and her allies know that the work of protecting the multiverse is far from over.

The final scene shows Zephyr Astra in the Celestial Aurora, looking up at the stars with determination. She is ready for new adventures, new challenges and the next phase of her interdimensional mission. The future is uncertain, but she is willing to face it.

The story closes with the image of the spaceship disappearing into the depths of interstellar space, suggesting that Zephyr Astra's journey is far from over, and that the multiverse still holds unknown secrets and dangers.

This open ending leaves room for future installments in the series and keeps readers intrigued and eager to find out what happens next in Zephyr Astra's exciting intergalactic journey.

Twist in Dimensions

After the epic confrontation with the Devourer of Realities and the sealing of the Gates of Chaos that he threatened, the Celestial Dawn departed for a seemingly peaceful dimension called Harmony. But the multiverse held surprises, and the next challenge was unlike anything I had faced.

Harmonia was a world of apparent peace, with floating cities and a serene atmosphere. However, something was wrong. The inhabitants of Harmonia, ethereal beings of light, were mysteriously disappearing, leaving behind a void of energy.

I was greeted by Syritha, the guardian of Harmony, who explained that the dimensional balance had been disrupted. A temporal distortion was causing Harmonia's own reality to collapse. It was a surprising turn of events, as the harmony that had previously reigned was now threatened.

My mission in Harmonia was to discover the source of the time distortion and restore balance. Syritha guided me through floating landscapes and stunning architecture, but also through voids where beings of light had disappeared.

The challenge in Harmonia was a complex temporal puzzle. I had to navigate through different moments in time and solve puzzles to understand how the distortion had started. Each answer led to more questions, and Harmonia's timeline seemed to fold in on itself.

Eventually, I discovered that an ancient artifact was at the center of the time distortion. It was a Cosmic Lyre, capable of manipulating time and space. Someone had unleashed his energy without understanding the consequences.

Using the wisdom gained from my previous journeys, I was able to reverse the temporal distortion and restore harmony in Harmony. The beings of light returned, and the floating city glowed with new energy.

Syritha thanked him gratefully, and the Celestial Dawn prepared to leave. I looked back, knowing that in each dimension, new challenges awaited. The interdimensional journey continued, and I was determined to face each twist and mystery with the courage and wisdom I gained along the way.

Song of the Stars

My next stop was Lyrithia, a world enveloped in music and poetry. This was a place where creativity flowed like a river of stars, and the landscape was filled with celestial instruments that resonated with cosmic sounds.

The Celestial Aurora landed in a city built in harmony with the rhythm of the stars. The streets were like sheet music, and the houses looked like musical instruments. The inhabitants, ethereal beings with wings that seemed to vibrate with musical notes, greeted me with soft melodies.

I was welcomed by Meliora, the guardian of Lyrithia, a serene composer of the stars. She explained to me that music was the essence of this world and that heavenly harmony was threatened by a growing dissonance.

The challenge in Lyrithia was linked to restoring the musical harmony that connected all dimensions. Meliora led me along cosmic trails and rivers of light, where the sounds of the stars were tangible. Every note, every melody was part of a great universal symphony.

I discovered that a dissonance was spreading, causing chaos in the cosmic music. It was like an out-of-tune note that contaminated all the others. I had to find the source of the dissonance and restore harmony.

Navigating through a sonic maze, I arrived at a dark chamber where a shadowy creature was trapped. It was the Incarnation of Dissonance, an entity that fed on musical chaos. Using an artifact of cosmic music, I enveloped it in a melody of pure harmony, weakening its influence.

The dissonance dissipated, and the symphony of stars came together in an explosion of light and sound. Meliora thanked her with a smile that blazed like a comet, and the city of Lyrithia celebrated with music that resonated throughout the cosmos.

I left Lyrithia with the sound of the stars still echoing in my ears. Each dimension he visited was unique, with its own challenges and wonders. The Celestial Aurora was ready for its next stop, and I knew the interdimensional adventure would continue, bringing new melodies and mysteries as I explored the multiverse.

The Garden of Whispers

The Celestial Aurora took me to a mysterious world called Whisperia, where secrets were whispered by gentle breezes and flowers carried stories in their delicate petals. It was a place of enchantment and mystery.

Upon landing in Whisperia, I was greeted by Aelarion, the guardian of this world. He was a being made of light and shadow, whose words were like melodies that danced through the air. Aelarion explained to me that in Whisperia, truths were revealed through the whispers of nature.

The challenge in this world was to decipher the whispers and uncover the secrets that had been kept for ages. The trees whispered old memories, and the flowers answered questions with their colorful petals.

I walked through the gardens of Whisperia, where the flowers whispered of lost loves and forgotten battles. The trees murmured about the past and the future, while the wind brought riddles that needed to be deciphered.

With each whisper, I came closer to understanding a deep secret, a cosmic truth that was hidden within Whisperia. I discovered that a mysterious artifact was at the center of it all, a Whispering Stone that had the power to reveal or hide truths.

Aelarion guided me to the Whispering Stone, and with the help of the secrets I had collected, I activated it. The Stone radiated light and shadow, and Whisperia's secrets were revealed.

But with the revelation came a choice. Some secrets were best left hidden, while others were crucial to understanding the multiverse. It was a difficult decision, but Aelarion's wisdom guided me to the right choice.

With Whisperia's secrets revealed and understood, Aelarion gave thanks and the Celestial Dawn led me forward. Each dimension I visited revealed a unique facet of the multiverse, and the search for knowledge and balance continued as I explored the mysteries the universe had to offer.

The Mirror of Truth

The Celeste dawn guided me to a world called Veridium, where truth was the driving force of all things. In this world, reality was reflected in magic mirrors, and lies were a distortion that unleashed chaos.

Upon landing in Veridium, I was greeted by Miriana, the guardian of truth. She was a majestic figure, with eyes that seemed to contain the pure essence of reality. Miriana explained to me that in Veridium, truth and lies had immediate and tangible consequences.

The challenge in Veridium was about understanding the truth and restoring balance. Each magical mirror reflected different realities, some beautiful and harmonious, others distorted and chaotic. It was my task to identify the distortions caused by the lie and restore the truth.

I walked through landscapes where mirrors revealed the history of individuals and civilizations. I discovered that a massive distortion was threatening Veridium, a lie that had spread like a plague and was distorting reality.

With Miriana's help, I located the source of the lie, an Artifact of Deception that was in the possession of a deceptive entity. I was challenged to confront the entity in a magic mirror, where truth and lies intertwined in a duel of words and perceptions.

The battle for the truth was intense, but with Miriana's guidance and deep understanding of the importance of truth, I was able to defeat the entity of deception and seal the Artifact. The lie undoes its distortions, and Veridium's reality is restored.

Miriana expressed her gratitude, and Aurora Celeste took me forward. Each dimension I visited taught me valuable lessons about the multiverse and its complex web of realities. The search for truth and balance was an ongoing journey, and I was ready to face the challenges that lay ahead.

The Symphony of Souls

The Celestial Dawn led me to a world known as Etherealis, where souls were the essence of everything. This was a place where spiritual energy manifested as a symphony of colors and sounds, and souls were the center of life.

Upon landing in Etherealis, I was greeted by Seraphia, the guardian of souls. She radiated an aura of peace and compassion, and her words were like musical notes that echoed in the souls of everyone who heard her. Seraphia explained that in Etherealis, souls were linked by threads of spiritual energy that formed a web of connections.

The challenge in this world was related to restoring harmony between souls who had lost their bonds. The spiritual energies had intertwined in a chaotic manner, causing conflicts and imbalances in the spiritual symphony of Etherealis.

I walked through fields where vibrant colors intertwined, representing souls and their connecting threads. The work was delicate and required understanding the stories and connections of each soul.

I discovered that a dark entity had fed on the disharmony of souls, creating a spiritual maelstrom that threatened to consume Etherealis. It was my task to undo the distorted strands of spiritual energy and restore the bonds between souls.

With Seraphia's loving guidance, I began to weave the spiritual threads back into harmony. It was a process that required empathy and understanding, as each soul had a unique story and its own spiritual scars.

As spiritual connections were restored, the symphony of colors and sounds grew in intensity, filling Etherealis with renewed energy. The dark entity was weakened by the restoration of souls, and with one last effort, I managed to seal it in a distant dimensional portal.

Seraphia thanked him with gratitude and a beaming smile. The Celestial Aurora prepared to depart, carrying me forward on my interdimensional journey. Each dimension I visited taught me about the complexity of souls and the spiritual connections that united the multiverse. The search for spiritual harmony was a sacred task, and I was willing to face any challenges that came my way.

The sands of Time

Aurora Celeste's next stop took me to Chronosia, a world where time flowed like sand between fingers. Here, the landscapes were made of giant clocks, and the past, present and future blended together in a magical way.

Upon landing in Chronosia, I was greeted by Cronius, the guardian of time. He was an imposing figure with a cloak that resembled a grandfather clock. Cronius explained that in Chronosia, temporal balance was threatened, and distortions in time caused strange confluences of events.

The challenge in Chronosia was related to restoring the flow of time and correcting temporal distortions. Cronius guided me through landscapes where past, present and future moments met in a chaotic way. It was my task to understand the nature of the distortions and bring back temporal order.

I walked through corridors of old clocks that marked the time of different realities. I discovered that a temporal anomaly was causing pivotal moments from multiple dimensions to collide, creating paradoxes that threatened the multiverse.

With Cronius' help, I traced the patterns of temporal distortions and identified the source of the anomaly: a Chaos Clock, a magical artifact that disrupted the flow of time.

I faced the Chaos Clock in a battle that defied the very notion of time. With each blow, time distorted, creating waves of paradoxes. But with Cronius' guidance, I was able to seal the artifact and restore the time flow.

Chronosia began to stabilize, and giant clocks began to keep time harmoniously again. Cronius expressed his gratitude, and the Celestial Dawn prepared to depart.

Each dimension I visited taught me about the complexity of time and its influence on the multiverse. The quest to restore temporal balance was a fascinating challenge, and I was ready to face the mysteries of time that were yet to come on my interdimensional journey.

Labyrinth of Emotions

The Celestial Aurora guided me to a world called Emothria, where emotions were intertwined with reality itself. This was a place where feelings were visible, and the landscapes were a reflection of people's emotions.

Upon landing in Emothria, I was greeted by Elysar, the guardian of emotions. He was an ethereal being whose aura changed color according to the emotions he felt. Elysar explained that in Emothria, emotions were the lifeblood of the world, but an emotional imbalance was causing storms of feelings.

The challenge in Emothria was related to restoring emotional balance and understanding the connections between emotions and reality. Elysar guided me through landscapes where emotions raged like storms and others vanished like fog.

I discovered that an entity called the Turbilion was feeding on the chaotic emotions and causing imbalance. It was my task to restore emotional harmony and face Turbilion to restore stability.

Sailing through the turbulent seas of emotions, I reached a culmination where Turbilion was gathering the distorted emotions. The battle was intense, as emotions materialized like elements of nature.

With Elysar's guidance and my growing understanding of emotions, I was able to neutralize Turbilion and bring emotional harmony back to Emothria. The storms of feelings calmed down, and the landscapes reflected an emotional serenity.

Elysar expressed his gratitude with a smile that radiated peace. The Celestial Dawn was ready to depart, and I knew that my interdimensional journey would continue to explore the complexities of emotions and their influence on reality.

Each dimension I visited taught me valuable lessons about the interconnectedness of emotions and reality, and I was ready to face the emotional challenges that were yet to come on my journey.

The Haven of Memories

The Celestial Dawn took me to a world called Memorian, where memories were the basis of all existence. Here, each memory formed the landscape and story of each individual, and a vast ocean of memories connected all souls.

Upon landing in Memorian, I was greeted by Memoros, the keeper of memories. He was an ethereal figure, with eyes that glowed with reminiscences of eons past. Memoros explained that in Memorian, memories were sacred, but a vortex of forgetfulness was threatening to erase the memories and unleash chaos.

The challenge in Memorian was related to preserving and restoring the memories that sustained the world. Memoros guided me through a landscape filled with floating books that contained the stories of each soul. It was my task to stop the vortex of forgetfulness from consuming these precious memories.

I walked through fields where fragments of memories floated like butterflies of light. I discovered that the vortex of forgetting was fueled by anguish and the fear of forgetting. To stop him, I had to bring back lost memories and restore the connection between souls and their stories.

With Memoros' guidance, I faced the vortex of forgetting in a battle that tested my ability to remember and honor memories. Each restored memory weakened the vortex, until finally it was sealed in a dimensional abyss.

Memorian stabilized again, and memories flowed freely, supporting the landscape and identity of each soul. Memoros expressed his gratitude with a solemn gesture, and Aurora Celeste prepared to leave.

Each dimension I visited taught me about the power and importance of memories in our existence. The quest to preserve these memories was a sacred responsibility, and I was ready to face the challenges that lay ahead on my interdimensional journey.

The Kingdom of Dreams

The Celestial Aurora took me to a world called Oneíria, where dreams were as real as waking life. This was a place where imagination flourished and the limits of reality were challenged at every moment.

Upon disembarking in Oneíria, I was greeted by Oneiros, the guardian of dreams. He was an ethereal presence, with eyes that glowed with the spark of creativity. Oneiros explained that in Oneíria, dreams were the substance of reality, but a storm of nightmares was threatening to consume everything.

The challenge in Oneíria was related to restoring harmony between dreams and reality. Oneiros guided me through dreamlike landscapes where imagination reigned and nightmares distorted the landscape. It was my task to unlock the secrets of dreams and face the storm of nightmares.

I walked through lands where landscapes changed according to people's imaginations and nightmares distorted reality. I discovered that a dark entity called Morphenon was feeding on the nightmares and threatening to consume Oneíria with darkness.

With Oneiros' guidance, I navigated the twisted dreams and faced Morphenon in a confrontation that defied my own imagination. Each nightmare overcome weakened Morphenon, until I finally managed to seal the dark entity in a world of nightmares.

Oneíria once again shone with the light of dreams, and creativity flourished in every corner. Oneiros expressed his gratitude with a deep bow, and the Celestial Dawn prepared to leave.

Each dimension I visited taught me about the power of imagination and the importance of dreams in our journey. The quest to restore dream harmony was a fascinating challenge, and I was ready to face the dream mysteries that were yet to come on my interdimensional journey.

The Kingdom of Shadows

The Celestial Aurora led me to a dark and enigmatic world called Umbrosia, where shadows were as tangible as light. Here, the duality between light and dark was a powerful force that shaped reality.

Upon landing in Umbrosia, I was greeted by Umbriel, the guardian of shadows. He was an enigmatic figure, with eyes that seemed to contain deep secrets. Umbriel explained that in Umbrosia, the balance between light and shadow was unbalanced, and the shadows had begun to swallow the light.

The challenge in Umbrosia was related to restoring the balance between light and shadow and understanding the duality that shaped the world. Umbriel guided me through landscapes where shadows danced like entities of their own, creating challenges and illusions.

I discovered that a dark entity called Nocturna was feeding on the imbalance between light and shadow, threatening to consume Umbrosia with endless darkness.

I walked through dark forests and cities lit only by moonlight, facing challenges that tested my understanding of duality. With Umbriel's guidance, I confronted Nocturna in a battle that unfolded against a backdrop of shadows and light.

With each step, I balanced light and shadow, weakening Nocturna and restoring balance. Finally, I managed to seal the dark entity into an abyss where duality was eternal.

Umbrosia once again found harmony between light and shadow, and the Celestial Aurora prepared to leave. Umbriel expressed her gratitude with a mysterious smile, and I knew that my interdimensional journey would continue to explore the complexities of the duality that shaped every reality.

Each dimension I visited taught me about the balance between light and shadow and how this duality was essential to understanding the multiverse. The quest to restore this balance was a fascinating challenge, and I was ready to face the mysteries that lay ahead on my journey.

The Land of the Elements

The Celestial Dawn took me to a world called Elementara, where the elements of nature were personified into powerful beings. This was a place where earth, water, fire, and air ruled the landscape, each with its own personality.

Upon landing in Elementara, I was greeted by Terraegis, the guardian of the elements. He was an imposing figure, with skin covered in stones and a serene gaze. Terraegis explained that in Elementara, the balance between the elements was threatened, and conflicts between them triggered natural catastrophes.

The challenge in Elementara was related to restoring balance between the elements and understanding their interdependence in creating reality. Terraegis guided me through landscapes where the earth trembled, the waters roared, the fire burned, and the air blew furiously.

I discovered that an elemental entity called Tempestus was causing distortions in the elements, triggering cataclysms. It was my task to bring harmony between the elements and face Tempestus to restore stability.

I walked through burning deserts, stormy seas, lush forests, and windy plains, facing challenges that tested my understanding of nature. With Terraegis' guidance, I confronted Tempestus in a battle that unfolded into a fusion of the elements.

With each step, I balanced the elements and weakened Tempestus, until I finally managed to seal the elemental entity in a dimensional vortex. Elementara once again found harmony between the elements, and the Celestial Aurora prepared to leave.

Terraegis expressed its gratitude with a gesture of reverence to nature, and I knew that my interdimensional journey would continue to explore the complexities of the elements that shaped each reality.

Each dimension I visited taught me about the interdependence of the elements and how they influenced the creation of each world. The quest to restore this balance was a fascinating challenge, and I was ready to face the mysteries that lay ahead on my journey.

The City of Harmony

The Celestial Aurora led me to a world called Harmony, where peace and balance were the essence of all existence. This was a place where differences were celebrated, and cooperation between beings of all kinds was valued.

Upon landing in Harmonia, I was greeted by Harmonius, the guardian of peace. He radiated calm and serenity, and his words were like gentle songs that soothed the soul. Harmonius explained that in Harmonia, a destructive conflict threatened to upset the balance, and differences between the inhabitants were becoming a source of discord.

The challenge in Harmonia was related to restoring peace and understanding the underlying causes of conflict. Harmonius guided me through cities where beings of different races and origins coexisted, but the tensions were palpable.

I discovered that a dark entity called Discordia was feeding on division and conflict, threatening to plunge Harmonia into destructive chaos.

I walked through squares where heated arguments turned into confrontations and differences of opinion became deep divisions. With Harmonius' guidance, I explored the roots of the conflict, speaking with inhabitants of Harmonia and seeking peaceful solutions.

By understanding the causes of conflict and promoting dialogue, I was able to weaken Discordia and focus attention toward harmony and collaboration. Finally, we sealed the dark entity in a space where discord had no voice.

Harmony bloomed again, and the Celestial Aurora prepared to leave. Harmonius expressed his gratitude with a gesture of peace, and I knew that my interdimensional journey would continue to explore the challenges of peace and coexistence.

Each dimension I visited taught me about the importance of harmony and mutual understanding, and I was ready to face the mysteries that were yet to come on my journey.

The Stars of Wisdom

The Celestial Aurora led me to a world called Astralis, where knowledge and wisdom were the greatest riches. This was a place where the stars were like cosmic libraries, and the secrets of the universe were waiting to be discovered.

Upon landing in Astralis, I was greeted by Astrus, the guardian of wisdom. He possessed an aura of intellectual luminosity and eyes that sparkled with the curiosity of knowledge. Astrus explained that in Astralis, the quest for knowledge was in danger, and forgetfulness threatened to extinguish the light of understanding.

The challenge in Astralis was related to the preservation of knowledge and the search for truth in the vast cosmos. Astrus guided me through starry skies where constellations were like ancient manuscripts, and comets carried hidden secrets.

I discovered that an entity called Ignoranta was obscuring the stars and causing knowledge to be lost in the shadows. It was my task to unlock the cosmic secrets and face Ignoranta to restore the light of wisdom.

I navigated through nebulas of confusion and black holes of ignorance, unraveling cosmic enigmas and rescuing lost knowledge. With Astrus's guidance, I faced Ignoranta in a battle of words and concepts, where understanding was the most powerful weapon.

With each revelation, I weakened Ignoranta, until I finally managed to seal the entity in the stellar vortex of oblivion. Astralis once again shone with the light of wisdom, and the Celestial Aurora prepared to depart.

Astrus expressed his gratitude with a bow to the vastness of knowledge, and I knew that my interdimensional journey would continue to explore the secrets of the universe and the tireless search for truth.

The Heart of Emotions

The Celestial Aurora took me to a world called Corallia, where emotions were the essence of all life. This was a place where emotional oceans and creatures that embodied feelings sailed through deep waters of feelings.

Upon landing in Corallia, I was greeted by Coralina, the guardian of emotions. She was a mermaid whose songs were made of pure emotion, and her skin glowed with the colors of emotional tides. Coralina explained that on Corallia, emotional balance was threatened, and devastating emotional storms hit the lands and seas.

The challenge in Corallia was related to restoring balance between emotions and understanding the importance of accepting and expressing feelings. Coralina guided me through reefs where emotional corals grew, and waves of joy and sadness met.

I discovered that an entity called Tormentia was causing uncontrolled emotional storms, feeding on the intensity of feelings. It was my task to calm the storms and face Tormentia to restore emotional harmony.

I sailed through seas of anger and calm, facing whirlwinds of intense emotions. With Coralina's guidance, I sought empathy and understanding the emotions of sea creatures that personified feelings. Through understanding, I was able to calm the emotional storms and weaken Tormentia.

Finally, I faced the entity in an emotional confrontation where empathy and balance were my most powerful weapons. With that, I managed to seal Tormentia into an emotional coral reef.

Corallia once again found harmony between her emotions, and Aurora Celeste prepared to leave. Coralina expressed her gratitude with a song that brought tears of joy to everyone who heard it, and I knew that my interdimensional journey would continue to explore the complexities of emotions and their influence on life.

Each dimension I visited taught me about the importance of understanding and embracing emotions, and I was ready to face the emotional challenges that were yet to come on my journey.

The Time Machine

THE AURORA CELESTE guided me to a world called Cronotech, where time and technology merged in a dance of gears and paradoxes. This was a place where time machines were as common as cars, and the past and future could be explored as if they were living museums.

Upon landing at Cronotech, I was greeted by Kronix, the guardian of time. He was an android whose eyes were visors that displayed events from all eras. Kronix explained that in Cronotech, a disruption in the timeline was causing temporal distortions, and paradoxes were arising frequently.

The challenge at Cronotech was related to restoring temporal integrity and understanding the ethical implications of messing with the past and future. Kronix guided me through cities where time machines were used for tourist time travel, but carelessness was causing problems.

I discovered that a company called TemporaCorp was exploiting the misuse of time machines, causing paradoxes that threatened temporal continuity. It was my task to resolve the paradoxes and face TemporaCorp to restore the timeline.

I traveled through historical moments, resolving paradoxes that had the potential to rewrite history. With Kronix's guidance, I understood the importance of preserving the past while looking to the future.

Finally, I confronted TemporaCorp in a battle that unfolded in a field of paradoxes. With an act of ethics and wisdom, I managed to seal the company in a dimension where time had no meaning.

Cronotech found temporal integrity again, and the Aurora Celeste prepared to depart. Kronix expressed his gratitude with a programmed nod, and I knew that my interdimensional journey would continue to explore the complexities of temporal manipulation.

Each dimension I visited taught me about the responsibilities of messing with time and the ethical implications of that action. The quest to restore the timeline was a fascinating challenge, and I was ready to face the mysteries of time that lay ahead on my journey.

Portal of Possibilities

Chapter 27: The Portal of Possibilities**

The Celestial Aurora led me to a world called Potentialia, where possibilities were endless and choices shaped reality. This was a place where dimensional portals opened in all directions, connecting dream worlds and alternate realities.

Upon landing in Potentialia, I was greeted by Potentius, the guardian of possibilities. He had a fluid appearance, as if he was constantly changing to adapt to the choices being made around him. Potentius explained that in Potentialia, freedom of choice was a gift and a responsibility, but an entity called the Limitora was trying to restrict the possibilities and create a single determined path.

The challenge in Potentialia was related to defending freedom of choice and understanding the power of decisions in our journey. Potentius guided me through portals that led to alternate realities, where different choices had created different results.

I discovered that Limitora was limiting people's freedom of choice, pushing them in predetermined directions. It was my task to challenge these restrictions and face Limitora to restore the multiplicity of possibilities.

I navigated portals of probability, exploring realities where different decisions had led to varying destinations. With Potentius' guidance, I understood that every choice we make creates a branch in the fabric of the multiverse.

Finally, I confronted Limitora in a clash of choices and possibilities. With the strength of freedom of choice and the understanding that every decision matters, I was able to seal the entity into a portal of infinite possibilities.

Potentialia shone again with the diversity of choices, and Aurora Celeste prepared to leave. Potentius expressed his gratitude with a smile that reflected all possible choices, and I knew that my interdimensional journey would continue to explore the power of decisions on our journey.

Each dimension I visited taught me about the importance of freedom of choice and how our decisions shape our destiny. The quest to restore the multiplicity of possibilities was a fascinating challenge, and I was ready to face the mysteries of choices that lay ahead on my journey.

End of the Journey

With all dimensions visited and restored, I returned to Aurora Celeste, knowing that my interdimensional journey was coming to an end. The skyship seemed more resplendent than ever, reflecting the colors and secrets of each world I visited.

As the ship rose into the skies between dimensions, I looked back at the realities I explored. Each contained valuable lessons about the nature of existence, the importance of memories, the power of dreams, the duality of light and shadow, the harmony of emotions, temporal integrity, and the multiplicity of possibilities.

Now, my journey was coming to an end, but the Celestial Aurora would continue to travel the multiverse in search of other dimensions that needed help. I knew that new guardians would emerge to face the challenges that the multiverse presented.

As the skyship drifted into the distance, I felt a deep sense of gratitude for having been part of this interdimensional adventure. I knew that my own journey was far from over, and that new horizons and mysteries awaited.

The grand finale of this story is open-ended, with countless possibilities for what will happen next. The Celestial Aurora continues to roam the multiverse, and who knows what challenges and adventures await the next guardians who embark on its journey. The multiverse is vast and full of secrets, and the starting point is just the beginning of an endless interdimensional journey.

Epilogue

After having explored countless dimensions and restoring balance in each of them, our heroine returns to the Celestial Aurora, with the knowledge and wisdom of all the realities she visited. The mysterious guardians who guided her on her interdimensional journey greet her with a look of approval, knowing that she has become a true protector of the multiverse.

The skyship continues its journey, leaving behind the dimensions that were saved, but knowing that new challenges await somewhere in the vast expanses of the multiverse. The heroine looks at the twinkling stars through the windows of Aurora Celeste and wonders what future adventures await not only her, but also the next guardians who will embark on this mission.

The multiverse is vast and infinite, full of mysteries and unexplored possibilities. Each dimension is a blank page waiting to be written, and the Celestial Aurora is the pen that shapes these interdimensional stories. As she continues her journey, new guardians will emerge, each with their own unique journey, but all united by the purpose of protecting the diversity of realities.

Our heroine looks at the starry horizon and smiles, knowing that her own journey is not yet over. She is also part of the multiverse, and her interdimensional adventures are just beginning. With a heart full of gratitude and determination, she prepares to face the mysteries and challenges that the multiverse holds, going beyond the stars in search of new frontiers and discoveries.

And so, the Celestial Aurora disappears into the depths of the multiverse, slipping between dimensions like a shooting star, leaving behind a trail of infinite possibilities. The story of the Guardians of the Dimensions continues, and the multiverse eagerly waits to reveal its secrets to the brave hearts who dare to explore it.

Afterword

** Afterword: The Multiverse of Possibilities**

In this afterword, I want to extend my deepest thanks to all of you, dear readers, for embarking on this interdimensional journey with me. Writing "Guardians of the Dimensions: The Interdimensional Journey" was an adventure in itself, and knowing that you have been along for the ride is truly rewarding.

In this story, we explore imaginary worlds, face epic challenges, and learn lessons about the nature of existence, the importance of choices, and the power of empathy. Each dimension visited represented an opportunity to explore deep concepts and, at the same time, delve into exciting adventures.

As we close this book, I invite all of you to reflect on the messages and lessons you have found within the interdimensional pages. Remember that, like the guardians of the Celestial Dawn, each of us is on our own journey, facing unique challenges and making choices that shape our destiny.

I deeply believe in the ability of each individual to make a difference in the world, just as our guardians did in each dimension they visited. May this story inspire you to embrace courage, wisdom, and empathy in your own journeys, no matter how challenging they may seem.

The multiverse is vast, full of unexplored possibilities, and life is an interdimensional adventure waiting to be experienced. Thank you for being part of this journey, and may your own paths be filled with exciting discoveries, wise choices, and, most of all, compassion for the universe we share.

With gratitude and admirable curiosity,
Antonio Carlos Pinto
08/28/2023

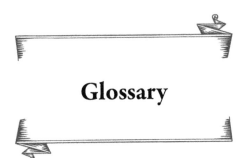

Glossary

Aurora Celeste : A mysterious celestial ship that travels the multiverse in search of dimensions in danger. She is the protagonist of the story and a guardian of realities.

Guardians of Dimensions : Individuals chosen by the Celestial Aurora to protect and restore balance in dimensions in danger.

Dimensions : Individual worlds with unique realities, each facing specific challenges throughout history.

Limiter : An entity that tries to restrict possibilities in the dimensions it visits, limiting freedom of choice.

Temporalia : A dimension where time and technology merge, and time machines are used to travel to the past and future.

TemporaCorp : A company that exploits the misuse of time machines, causing distortions in the timeline.

Cronotech : The world where the Temporalia dimension is found.

Discordia : A dark entity that feeds on divisions and conflicts in the dimensions it visits.

Harmonius : The guardian of the Harmony dimension, responsible for maintaining peace and balance.

Harmony : A dimension where peace and cooperation between beings of all races are valued, but where conflicts threaten the balance.

Ignoranta : An entity that obscures the stars in Astralis, causing forgetfulness and loss of knowledge.

Astrus : The guardian of the Astralis dimension, responsible for preserving knowledge and wisdom.

Astralis: A dimension where stars are like cosmic libraries, and knowledge of the universe is highly valued.

Tormentia : An entity that creates emotional storms in Corallia, feeding on the intensity of emotions.

Coralina : The guardian of the Corallia dimension, whose songs are made of pure emotion.

Corallia: A dimension where emotions are the essence of all life, and emotional oceans flow freely.

Potentius : The guardian of the Potentialia dimension, where possibilities are endless and choices shape reality.

Potentialia : A dimension where dimensional portals open to infinite possibilities, but where an entity called the Limiter attempts to restrict choices.

Multiverse : The set of all existing dimensions and realities, each with its own history and unique characteristics.

Interdimensional Journey : The epic adventure of the guardians of the Celestial Dawn to protect and restore balance in the different dimensions of the multiverse.

Oblivion : A threat that occurs when knowledge and memories are erased from a dimension, causing cultural and intellectual decline.

Paradoxes Temporals : Contradictory results and timeline distortions that occur when time machines are used inappropriately.

Freedom of Choice : The principle that individual decisions have the power to shape the destiny and reality of a dimension.

Realities Alternatives : Dimensions where different choices led to different results, creating parallel realities.

Diversity of Cosmos : The recognition of the richness and importance of the different realities and dimensions that exist in the multiverse.

Light and Shadow : Concept that refers to the duality between good and evil, balance and imbalance in the dimensions visited by the guardians.

Guardians Mysterious : Figures that guide and assist the guardians of the Celestial Aurora in each dimension, sharing wisdom and direction.

Mysterious Multiverse : The understanding that the multiverse is vast and filled with unsolved mysteries, inviting adventurers to explore the unknown.

Realities in Danger : Dimensions that face existential challenges, such as threats to their culture, history, emotional, temporal or choice balance.

Adventure Interdimensional : The unique journey the guardians embark on, facing dangers and unraveling enigmas in each dimension visited.

Borders of the Multiverse : The margins between dimensions, often represented by cosmic portals, where realities intertwine and connect.

Fate of the Multiverse : The result of the guardians' actions and the choices they make, shaping the future and diversity of the multiverse as a whole.

Star Writing : The poetic concept that the universe is an ever-evolving narrative, and that every action of the guardians is like a word in the cosmic story.

Eternal Dawn : The idea that the Celestial Aurora will continue its interdimensional journey indefinitely, protecting and exploring new realities.

This glossary aims to enrich the understanding of the complex dimensions and concepts explored in this interdimensional story, inviting readers to delve into the depths of the multiverse and its countless facets.

Appendices

I n this appendix, we present a more detailed look at the dimensions explored in the story "Star Exodus: The Lost Dimension". Each dimension is unique in its challenges, culture and characteristics, providing a wide range of interdimensional experiences.

1. Harmony
- Guardian: Harmonius
- Challenge: Preserve peace and balance in a dimension where conflicts threaten harmony.
- Characteristics: A diverse society of peaceful beings who value cooperation and understanding.

2. Ignorant
- Guardian: Astrus
- Challenge: Deal with the threat of oblivion, where knowledge and memories are disappearing.
- Characteristics: A society that fights to preserve its cultural and historical heritage.

3. Corallia
- Guardian: Coralina
- Challenge: Face emotional storms that threaten the stability of emotions.
- **Features:** A dimension where emotions are the basis of life, with vast emotional oceans.

4. Temporalia
- Guardian: TemporaCorp

- Challenge: Control time machines and avoid temporal paradoxes.
- Characteristics: A society where time and technology intertwine, allowing temporal travel.

5. Astralis
   - Guardian: Ignoranta
   - Challenge: Face the darkness that obscures the stars and threatens knowledge.
   - **Features:** A dimension where stars are sources of cosmic knowledge.

6. Discord
   - Guardian: Unknown
   - Challenge: Deal with the entity Discordia and its destructive effects on society.
   - Features: A dimension where chaos and discord are prevalent.

7. Potentialia
   - Guardian: Potentius
   - Challenge: Navigate between countless possibilities and infinite choices.
   - Features: A dimension where dimensional portals open to a multiverse of options.

Each dimension offers a rich tapestry of challenges and opportunities, and the guardians of the Celestial Dawn must adapt their skills and knowledge to face these unique realities. This interdimensional exploration is a celebration of the diversity of the multiverse and the incredible adaptability of the human spirit.

About the author

Prepare to embark on a journey that transcends the boundaries of our known universe.

Meet Antonio Carlos Pinto, a 40-year-old author, born in the picturesque municipality of Maranguape, in the State of Ceará, Brazil. But Antonio is much more than a writer - he is an interdimensional visionary, a master of science fiction and fantasy, and an inspiring example of resilience.

Born with autism, Antonio faced challenges that many of us cannot imagine. However, he turned this unique journey into a source of extraordinary strength and creativity. Your mind is a portal to worlds beyond the stars, where entire galaxies dance in cosmic harmony and imagination knows no limits.

As we delve into the pages of his stories, we are taken on an intergalactic odyssey, guided by Antonio's skillful writing and his unparalleled ability to create vibrant universes and unforgettable characters. Each word is a shooting star, lighting the way into the unknown and challenging our own perceptions of what is possible.

Antonio gives us a rare glimpse into the complexities of the multiverse, where the Guardians of Light face the Unknown Shadows in a battle that transcends time and space. Its narrative envelopes us with a symphony of emotion, mystery and courage, reminding us that, even in the farthest reaches of the cosmos, humanity finds its own essence.

As we turn each page, we are transported not just to new worlds, but to new perspectives. Antonio Carlos Pinto challenges us to look beyond the stars, beyond limitations, and to embrace the truth that imagination is truly our vehicle to eternity.

Not only are we witnessing the rise of an exceptional autistic author, but we are connecting with an explorer of the unknown, an architect of universes, and a visionary whose impact will resonate through the ages.

Prepare yourself for a journey that transcends imagination. Prepare yourself for Antonio Carlos Pinto, the interdimensional visionary whose words will guide us beyond time and space. ◇◇◇

Don't miss out!

Visit the website below and you can sign up to receive emails whenever Antonio Carlos Pinto publishes a new book. There's no charge and no obligation.

https://books2read.com/r/B-A-RODAB-TJIQC

BOOKS 2 READ

Connecting independent readers to independent writers.

Did you love *Stellar Exodus and the Lost Dimension*? Then you should read *Êxodo Estelar e A Dimensão Perdida*[1] by Antonio Carlos Pinto!

[2]

Na encruzilhada das distorções cronotemporais, entre dobras estelares e galáxias entrelaçadas por singularidades quânticas, revela-se um multiverso de estruturas cognitivas elevadas. Uma tapeçaria exponencial de realidades fractais, onde espaçonaves são âncoras da transcognição, entrelaçando-se em danças quânticas.

Sob o égide da Aurora Celeste, Zephyr Astra se torna o vetor cognitivo, navegando pelos pliegues da existência. Portais são umbrais de consciência, aberturas nas tessituras do tempo-espaço.

Em cada planície dimensional, a gravidade da possibilidade é transmutada por leis fluidas da física cognitiva. Zephyr enfrenta não

---

1. https://books2read.com/u/3GGQBQ

2. https://books2read.com/u/3GGQBQ

somente dilemas tridimensionais, mas eclosões fractais de potencialidade.

Esta é uma odisseia sem precedentes, uma busca pelo entendimento em um cosmos de complexidade insondável. O céu é uma abstração para aqueles que decifram os arcanos do continuum. A Aurora Celeste é a quintaessência da exploração, e o universo, um infinito de compreensão emergente.

Read more at https://www.amazon.com.br/Antonio-Carlos-Pinto/e/B08ZYRK243/ref=aufs_dp_mata_mbl.

About the Author

Antonio Carlos Pinto é um escritor apaixonado pelo ofício de criar histórias de ficção científica e fantasia. Sua vocação para a escrita surgiu já na infância e se consolidou ao longo dos anos por meio de muito estudo e dedicação à escrita.

Especializado em livros de ficção científica, fantasia e romances épicos de aventura, Antonio tem uma habilidade singular para transportar os leitores para outros mundos, sejam eles reais ou imaginários. Entre seus livros mais conhecidos estão A Feiticeira de Shadowthorn, Wastervale e Todos os Amores.

Sua escrita fluida e envolvente remete tanto a tempos antigos quanto a cenários futuristas. Antonio domina a língua portuguesa e suas nuances, o que lhe permite elaborar tramas complexas e textos ricos em detalhes.

Além de livros para o público adulto, Antonio também escreve ficção peculiar para os jovens leitores. Suas histórias cativantes incentivam o gosto pela leitura entre adolescentes.

Com sua imaginação fértil e seu talento primoroso para a narrativa, Antonio Carlos Pinto segue firme em seu propósito de levar ao público obras instigantes, que divertem e emocionam seus leitores.

Read more at https://www.amazon.com.br/Antonio-Carlos-Pinto/e/B08ZYRK243/ref=aufs_dp_mata_mbl.

About the Publisher

Antonio Carlos Pinto é um escritor dotado de uma mente criativa que sempre esteve imersa no poder das palavras. Sua incursão na arte da escrita teve início na infância, quando sua paixão por contar histórias começou a ganhar forma. À medida que os anos passaram, dedicou-se incansavelmente a aprimorar suas habilidades literárias.

Ele deseja compartilhar um pouco sobre seu estilo de escrita, que considera singular e inovador. Em suas obras, busca infundir vida nos personagens e nas narrativas através de uma abordagem que denomina "Sombroespério".

Esse estilo não se limita a uma única categoria, permitindo-lhe explorar ficção científica e dark fantasia, romance e poesia, assim como temas relacionados à religiosidade e espiritualidade.

A raiz do "Sombroespério" não repousa apenas na imaginação, mas sim na fusão de diversos estilos literários. Anteriormente, suas narrativas amalgamavam elementos dos estilos Gótico, Romântico,

Modernista e Pós-Modernista, dando origem ao que ele denominava "Neo-Romantismo Sombrio".

Esse estilo almejava combinar a intensidade emocional do Romantismo com a atmosfera sombria e elementos sobrenaturais do Gótico. Ademais, incorporava técnicas de narrativa fragmentada e a exploração da subjetividade do Modernismo, juntamente com elementos metaficcionais e a desconstrução narrativa do Pós-Modernismo.

A inserção de convenções tradicionais shakespearianas culminou na gênese do "Sombroespério". Essa sinergia entre o Neo-Romantismo Sombrio e o estilo característico de Shakespeare resulta em uma expressão literária ímpar e inovadora.

"Sombroespério" espelha a profundidade emocional do Neo-Romantismo Sombrio e a eloquência dramática de Shakespeare, criando uma abordagem que desafia e comove o leitor.

Antonio Carlos Pinto espera que essa breve introdução ao seu estilo de escrita tenha sido esclarecedora e aguarda ansiosamente para compartilhar mais sobre suas obras e explorar as possibilidades de colaboração.